TO: BUSTA

FROM: MARGI xxoo

Runaway Bear

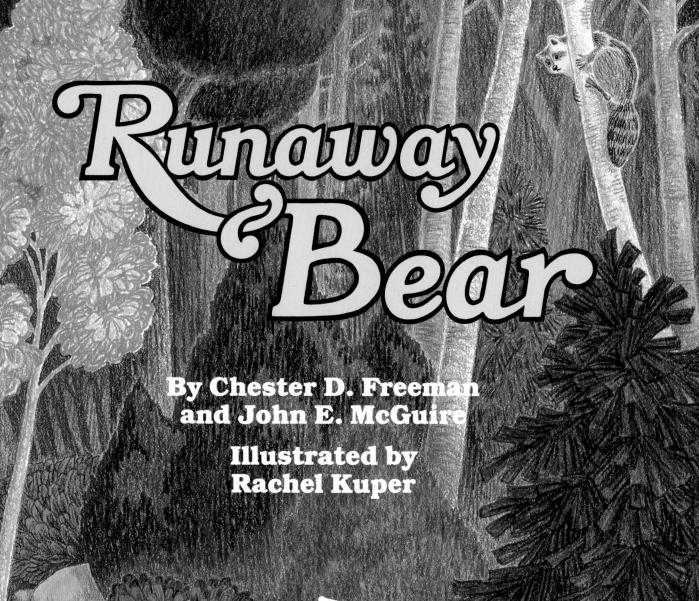

Runaway Bear

By Chester D. Freeman
and John E. McGuire

Illustrated by
Rachel Kuper

PELICAN PUBLISHING COMPANY
Gretna 1993

For our parents.

The word "Pelican" and the depiction of a pelican are
trademarks of Pelican Publishing Company, Inc., and are
registered in the U.S. Patent and Trademark Office.

Library of Congress Cataloging-in-Publication Data

Freeman, Chester D.
    Runaway bear / by Chester D. Freeman and John E. McGuire ;
illustrations by Rachel Kuper.
        p.   cm.
    Summary: After a father lovingly creates two lifelike bears for
his twin daughters' birthday, one bear disappears before the big day
and must be rescued by his companion and some friendly animals.
    ISBN 0-88289-956-2
    [1. Teddy bears--Fiction. 2. Animals--Fiction. 3. Birthdays-
-Fiction.] I. McGuire, John E. II. Kuper, Rachel, ill.
III. Title.
PZ7.F87465Ru 1993
[E]--dc20   93-16893
                                                                  CIP
                                                                   AC

Manufactured in Hong Kong

Published by Pelican Publishing Company, Inc.
1101 Monroe Street, Gretna, Louisiana 70053

RUNAWAY BEAR

A long time ago, there lived a jeweler named James. Unfortunately, he had very little money. The rich and famous never went shopping in his neighborhood, so he had to content himself with common materials and projects.

One day, he remembered that his twin daughters were about to have a birthday. "This time," he said to his wife Matilda, "I want to do something very special for them! I saw a teddy bear in the window of the emporium, and I thought that it would be a fine gift for the girls."

"That's not a bad idea," said Matilda, "but aren't they rather expensive?"

"Yes, they are," said James. "But I was thinking—how hard could it be to make one?"

His wife gave him a big smile and said, "With all the tools in your shop, I believe you could make a teddy bear that is as lively as a *real* bear!"

After he closed his shop that very evening, he began to work on the birthday gifts. He made gears, joints, and even voice boxes that made some friendly growl sounds. He went back to his shop to work many late nights while his two children slept; and by day, he carefully hid the parts.

Finally, the time arrived to create the bears themselves. Unable to use real gold, he chose a gold-colored fur for the first bear. To make the other bear different, he chose brown fur.

The joints he labored over worked perfectly, and the growlers were so small that they would be undetected when the bears were squeezed.

At last, with the fur sewn and the bears assembled, the jeweler had only to stuff them. He stopped at the local sawmill and filled a sack with sawdust from the floor; then he rushed back to his shop and poured the sawdust into the bears. The limp piles of fur took shape, and the bears began to look like real animals.

Exhausted from all his work, and in his haste to go home, James forgot to put away his bears. After he locked the door, he glanced through the window and saw what he had done. There were only a few hours left to sleep, so he decided to just continue on his way. Then a strange feeling overtook him. He thought, for a moment, that he had seen the bears turn their heads to watch him as he walked down the street. "Impossible!" he said. "Yet when I put their shoe-button eyes in place, I did feel as if they were watching me. That just can't be. I must be overtired."

Shaking his head, he continued home and went upstairs. He went to bed quietly, so he would not wake Matilda and the children. As he drifted off to sleep, his mind began to wander in a dream. He seemed to be a visitor in his own shop. There were the two bears he had made, still sitting on his workbench.

To his surprise, the gold bear stretched out his arms, flexed his paws, and slowly moved his legs. James almost woke up in shock.

Suddenly, the gold bear pushed the brown bear with his paw, and out of his stitched mouth came, "Wake up!"

He poked him again, and this time he heard, "Stop that! It hurts! You're shifting my sawdust."

The jeweler could not believe his eyes or his ears. The two bears not only moved, but they talked!

He watched as the bears moved about the workbench, looking in the drawers. "What a wonderful world this is!" the brown bear said. "When we are given to the children, we will enjoy lots of adventures, but I don't think anything can be any nicer than this!"

"Maybe you can poke around in all this junk," said the gold bear, "but I'm bored. You can wait around to see the world, but not me!"

"Well, well!" thought James. "I created you out of all that junk." His dreamed-filled eyes burned with anger.

The gold bear pushed some boxes across the floor, and stacked them up with some difficulty.

"Clever fellow," the jeweler thought.

Without a moment's hesitation, the gold bear scampered up the boxes and pushed open the mail slot.

He squeezed himself
through the slot. He strained
and shifted his sawdust, then
with a big push, he was hanging
on the outside. "Are you coming
or not?" he shouted.

"No," came the small voice
from inside.

So the gold bear let go and
slid down the outside of the door.
As he hit the step, all of his sawdust seemed to settle into his
bottom. This momentary stress
broke a stitch in the sewing, and
little by little, the gold bear
began to lose his filling.

Not watching where he was going, the gold bear fell into the road with a soft thump. A small cloud of sawdust puffed out of the broken seam, but he was so intent on seeing the world that he did not notice. The village streets were deserted so late at night, and his little legs quickly carried him out of sight of the jeweler's shop. James felt drawn to follow him.

Shortly, the gold bear found himself at the edge of town. He began to run toward the forest that beckoned him.

"Wait!" shouted James. Suddenly he woke up from his dream. His loud shout awakened the whole household. "Go back to sleep. It was just a bad dream." he explained. But James had a hard time getting back to sleep, so he watched the sun come up. "Impossible," he thought. "Toys don't come to life, no matter how well made they are. Or do they?"

Hurriedly, the jeweler dressed and was off to work. He opened the door of his shop, only to stumble over a stack of boxes. "Hmmm," he said, "I thought I put these away." Then his eyes came to rest on his workbench. There sat his beautiful brown bear, all alone. The gold bear was nowhere in sight.

Sadly, he picked up the brown bear, holding him ever so tightly. Tears began to roll down his cheeks and splash on the furry little face. The bear seemed to hold on to his maker and give him comfort. James even thought the little arms had moved to hold him, but he decided that his tears had created the illusion.

"What shall I do?" he thought. "I wanted each of my children to have a special teddy bear, and now one is stolen. I don't know how a thief could have gotten in, but that seems to be the only logical explanation."

He summoned the constable and told his story. The constable listened carefully because they were friends. The evidence did not seem to add up. There were no open doors and no broken windows—only a pile of boxes.

"Perhaps you are overworked and you misplaced the bear. I'm sure he is here or at home. Toys don't run away," the constable said reassuringly. The jeweler recalled his dream and once again dismissed it.

He halfheartedly continued to look around throughout the day. Not able to make another bear in time, he thought that perhaps with something extra on the brown bear, his children could share the gift. They were generous with each other.

Spotting a small basket in his shop, he sewed bright-colored ribbon straps on it and fashioned a tiny backpack for the brown bear.

"There," he said after placing it on the bear. "One child can move his arms and legs, and the other can pack the basket." It was not like another bear, but it would simply have to do. Exhausted and sad, he put the teddy bear with his backpack basket in a brown paper bag, locked the door, and went home with the bag tucked under his arm. As soon as he entered the house, he rushed to the bedroom and hid the bag under the bed.

The children's excitement on the eve of their birthday made him a little uncomfortable. Would they like the bear?

That night, when the house was quiet, the birthday bear began to move in his bag. He vowed that each girl would have her own gift. Luckily, the bedroom door was unlatched, and he gently pushed it open. Then he walked toward the stairs to find his way out of the house. He was determined to find his friend and bring him home.

On the door that led outside, he noticed a flap at the bottom. All of a sudden, the flap opened and in walked an animal. The chase was on. Around the room and through the flap the terrified bear skidded and stumbled. He barely got away from the cat when he found himself entering a wooded area. "Surely I can hide here," he told himself. "Thank goodness my legs worked so well!"

The brown bear saw a bird trying to catch a worm. "Have you seen another bear like me?"

"Bear, you say!" exclaimed the bird. "How could I forget him? He made some mean remarks about my home. I hope you realize that my nest is a masterpiece of construction: a symphony of sticks, leaves, threads, feathers, and mud. I built it myself, and that bear laughed at it! I didn't tell him that he was losing his stuffing because he was acting so smart that he never let me talk—he did all the talking."

"That's my friend," the brown bear thought. He found the word "friend" a bit hard to use because friends do not pick on people, or even birds.

"I know the one," said another voice from a tree at the edge of the clearing. "I couldn't help overhearing. Go down past those blueberry bushes, and between those two big trees. You'll have a tight squeeze, but he could slip right through. In fact, he looked as if he hadn't had a good meal in a month! Maybe that's why he called me 'fatso'." The speaker paused to fluff out the fur on his portly body. "And of course, he had the usual things to say about my mask."

Apologizing for his friend, the brown bear now knew he was on his trail.

Sure enough, he could see a little trail of sawdust that glistened in the light of the night. The brown bear followed it through the woods, and it was getting easier and easier to spot. How much stuffing could his friend possibly have left? He must have been so busy finding fault with everyone he met that he had not realized what was wrong with himself.

"Am I going to be too late?" the brown bear asked himself as he broke into a run along the path. The sky was brightening with the first glow before sunrise, and he could see plainly that the sawdust led down to the edge of a marshy pond. And there it ended.

A glossy head glided over through the water and said, "Well, well, another one!"

"Another one? Then you've seen my friend?" the brown bear almost shouted.

"He needed to get across the pond, and he acted so nice. I helped him across," said the beaver. "Once he was over there, he began to make fun of my front teeth!"

"Thank you for helping my friend," said the brown bear. "Would you help me across the water too?"

The beaver smiled, paddled closer, and stretched out his broad, flat tail. The bear sat down on it cautiously and rode to the other side.

As he walked up the opposite bank, he tripped and toppled over on a pile of something in the grass.

"Ouch!" cried the something in a weak voice.

Horrified, the brown bear looked into the grass and saw all that remained of his poor friend. The brown bear began to retrace his steps, collecting what sawdust he could find and putting it into his backpack basket. "It doesn't look as if we'll have enough of this now."

"Oh please! Try to find help to put me back together! I'll do anything you say . . . anything!"

Suddenly, out of the sky overhead came the the call of a bird, "Over this way! I've found them." The beaver and the raccoon came puffing up the slope to offer their help.

The gold bear looked at all their faces, and whispered, "You're really going to help me after the way I—well, I wasn't very—you know what I mean."

"The way I look at it," the raccoon said, "I'd rather have a friend than an enemy any day."

So the beaver made two basketfuls of fine wood chips, and the bird flew in some of the softest feathers and pieces of string from her nest. The raccoon took it all, bit by bit, in his skillful fingers and stuffed it in through the open seam. Slowly, the gold bear began to look like himself again. At last, the bird used a strand of thread in her sharp beak to sew up the opening.

The gold bear's body looked plump and hearty, but his face still sagged with shame. "I can't thank you enough," he said in a small voice. "I am sorry."

All the animals helped their new friends back across the pond, and the bears went home. Before they lifted the door flap and slipped inside, the brown bear made his friend promise to listen for a change, and never to speak out loud if he could possibly avoid it.

Past the sleeping cat, up the stairs, and into the brown paper bag they crept.

As the sun spread its golden rays across the bedroom wall, the children knocked at the door. "Papa! Mama! Are you awake?"

"We are now, our birthday girls, come on in."

They bounced in and landed on the bed. With a brave smile, their father reached down and handed them the big brown paper bag.

As the children dumped the contents of the bag onto the bed, the jeweler gasped to see two bears tumble out— one brown bear with a backpack basket on his shoulders and a gold bear. "It can't be!" he thought to himself. But there it was, and there was no time to consider the matter further because he was too busy being hugged.